PIG the Rebel

Aaron Blabey

SCHOLASTIC INC.

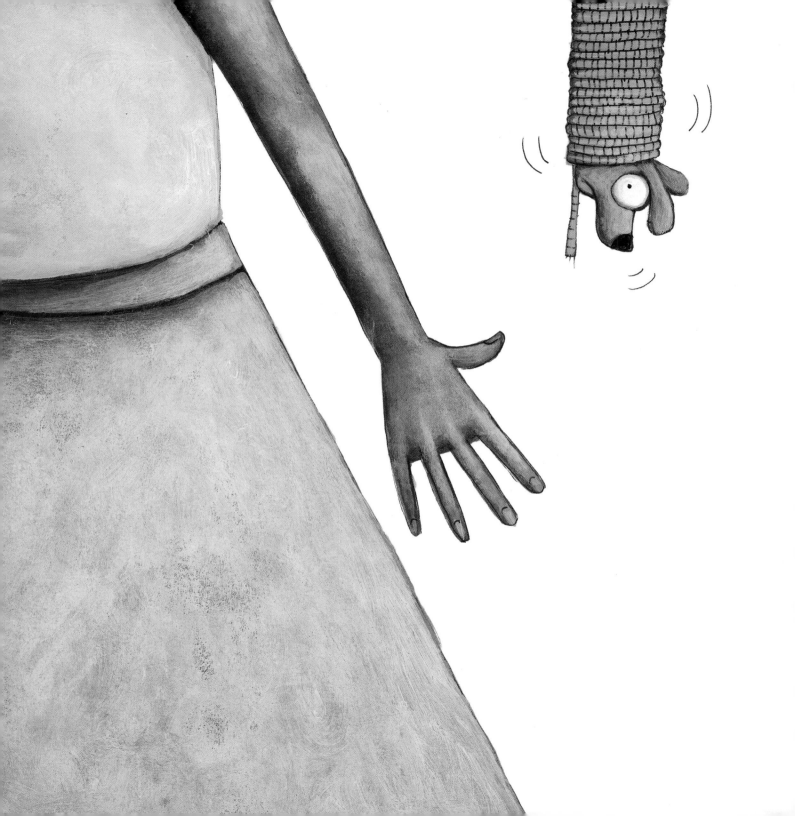

BIG JEAN'S
DOG OBEDIENCE SCHOOL

Certificate of Completion

AWARDED TO: PIG   BREED: PUG

FOR ACHIEVING GOOD BEHAVIOR

FAIL

*Dog trainer
since 1978*

SUCCESS RATE
100%
GUARANTEED!

*No job
too tough*

For the stars over Woodbury St.

First published in Australia in 2022 by Scholastic Press,
an imprint of Scholastic Australia Pty Ltd.

All rights reserved. Published by Scholastic Inc.,
Publishers since 1920. SCHOLASTIC and associated
logos are trademarks and/or registered trademarks of Scholastic Inc.

ISBN 978-1-338-86486-1

10 9 8 7 6 5 4 3 2   22 23 24 25 26

Printed in the U.S.A.   40
This edition first printing, September 2022

The artwork in this book is acrylic (with pens and pencils) on watercolor paper.
The type was set in Adobe Caslon.

Pig was a pug
and I'm sorry to say,
after years of his antics
it was now time to pay.

Yes, Pig was condemned
to a fate oh so cruel —
it was time for the dreaded . . .

The no-nonsense trainer
looked Pig up and down.
"I hear you've been naughty,"
she said with a frown.

She listed his crimes,
each wretched endeavor.
Pig pleaded *innocence*,
"What?! Who, *me*?
NEVER!"

- WON'T SHARE
- DISHONEST
- BAD SPORT
- BIT SANTA
- SHOW-OFF
- REFUSES TO BAT
- LAZY
- CULTURALLY IN
- RUINED
  HALLOWEE

"Hush!" said the trainer.
Her manner was gruff.
"Once you're done *here*,
you'll behave soon enough."

His class was a mixture of various mutts.
They all had their issues.
Some hyper. Some nuts.

A gall'ry of rogues!
A real motley crew!

"What are you in for?"

"I'm *bonkers*.
And you?"

"CLASS!" roared the trainer. "YOU WILL NOW LEARN TO **SIT!**"

SIT

Something in Pig *snapped* . . .

He bellowed, *"THAT'S IT!*

NO SCHOOL CAN CONTAIN ME!

LET'S BUST OUT OF HERE!"

His classmates were stunned,
but they gave a great cheer!

He mounted his steed
and they galloped apace.
But his steed lost its footing . . .

and fell on its face.

Pig found his feet, though.
With startling ferocity,
he hurtled downhill
at amazing velocity.

CAKES

He took out a cake stall.
Oh, how those cakes flew!

He took out the
hot dog guy's
new barbecue . . .

His escape was a triumph!
It really was. Yep!

But wait! Hang on!
What's this . . . ?

Hey, watch that last step!

The gas tank went

BOO

OM!

The sky filled with fur.
It looked like the end.
Oh, it sure did, yes sir.

What happened next?
Oh, how ends the book?
Do you dare turn the page?
Friends, *do you dare look*?

Who could survive
an explosion that BIG?!

Well . . .

. . . one slightly barbecued
potbellied PIG.

These days it's different,
I'm happy to say.

You've heard this before,
but hey, anyway . . .

His fur all grew back
(he did not need a wig),
and somehow that blast
blew some sense into Pig.

It sparked a new wisdom.
A new way of living —
devoting his future to
sharing and giving.

I know what you're thinking —
"He's fooling you, kid.
He'll NEEEEEEVER change!"

But guess what?

He did.

With love and thanks
to all of you. xo